This book
belongs to

....

....

First published 1995 by
Chart Books Limited, Chart Warren,
Seal, Sevenoaks, Kent. TN15 0EJ

ISBN 1-899912-07-X hardback
ISBN 1-899912-08-8 paperback

British Library Cataloguing in Publication Data
A catalogue record for this book is available from the British Library

Printed in Italy

TALES FROM HENRY'S GARDEN
MUGGERIDGE THE MOWER

WRITTEN BY SIMON HICKES

ILLUSTRATED BY JILL BROOKS

CHART BOOKS

Muggeridge was a mighty mower. He had a strong and powerful engine.

He had been in the shed for many years and had done a magnificent job keeping the lawn short and neat.

Muggeridge enjoyed his weekly task when Henry, the gardener, checked his petrol tank and with one pull of his starting cord, his blades whirred and his engine roared.

Moving up and down the garden, Muggeridge felt proud of the straight lines he cut. He was happy with his work.

The day came when Henry found it difficult to start Muggeridge. Muggeridge knew he was getting older. Sadly, the gardener put him back in the shed.

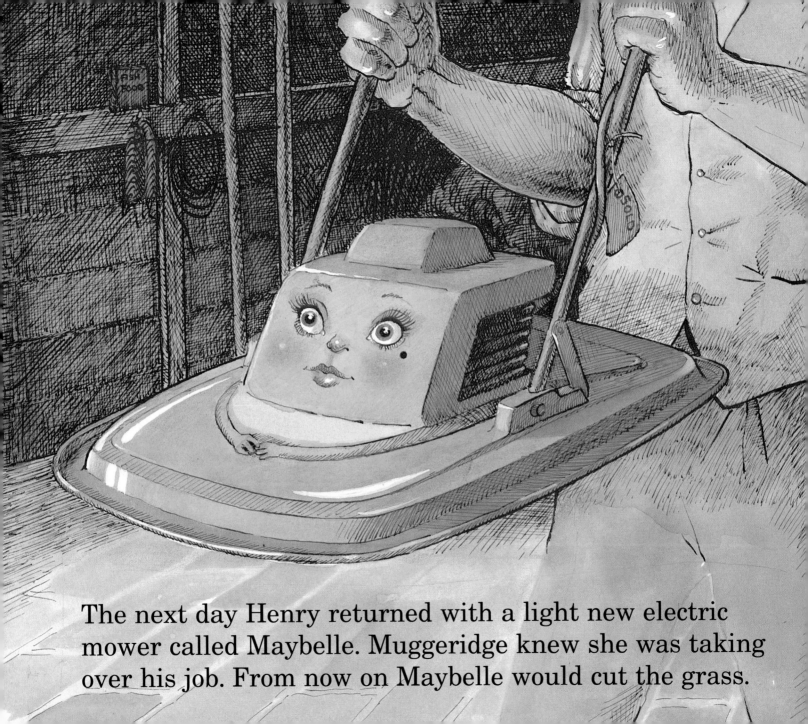

The next day Henry returned with a light new electric mower called Maybelle. Muggeridge knew she was taking over his job. From now on Maybelle would cut the grass.

Poor Muggeridge was gathering dust. He felt sad
inside. Spiders' webs were collecting on him. He
lost his sparkle.

In the middle of the summer there was to be a party in the garden. The grass had grown so long Maybelle got stuck!

To his surprise Muggeridge was taken out of the shed. His engine was cleaned thoroughly. Each blade was freshly oiled. Muggeridge felt his old self.

The time came to start up. When his cord was yanked there was a clattering, clunking sound followed by a thundering roar that shook the ground. Muggeridge was ready to go.

It was a challenge even for Muggeridge to cut
the long grass. Everybody agreed he had done a
splendid job. Muggeridge felt happy. He was pleased
that he could still be of use.

On the day of the party the lawn looked superb.
Maybelle would still cut the grass each week.
Muggeridge was used for special occasions.

Muggeridge was still a
"mighty mower!"

FURTHER

TALES FROM HENRY'S GARDEN

RUMBLES THE ROLLER
WILLIE THE WATERING CAN
SPIRO THE SPADE